For
Grandma Robin
and
the little ones in my life:
Theo, Sonia, Asha, Zilla & Iggy

THIS IS A BORZOI BOOK PUBLISHED BY ALFRED A. KNOPF

Copyright © 2018 by Phoebe Wahl
All rights reserved. Published in the United States by Alfred A. Knopf,
an imprint of Random House Children's Books,
a division of Penguin Random House LLC, New York.

Knopf, Borzoi Books, and the colophon are registered trademarks
of Penguin Random House LLC.

Library of Congress Cataloging-in-Publication Data is available upon request.
ISBN 978-1-5247-1527-4 (trade) — ISBN 978-1-5247-1528-1 (lib. bdg.) — ISBN 978-1-5247-1529-8 (ebook)

The illustrations in this book were created using watercolor, gouache, collage, and colored pencil.

MANUFACTURED IN CHINA
March 2018 10 9 8 7 6 5 4 3 2 1 First Edition

BACKYARD FAIRIES

By
Phoebe Wahl

Alfred A. Knopf   New York

Have you ever found,

while out on your own...

A tiny, magical somebody's home?

Or sensed a fluttering, flickering flight...

gone when you turn, just out of sight?

Or heard a little trill or tone?

Or seen a SUSPICIOUS-LOOKING stone?

Maybe one morning you wake up to see
that the dog's hair was braided
by somebody wee.

You might leave an offering,
then you discover,
it's vanished by morning,
replaced with another.

Have you ever woke up
when the moon is round
and crept out of bed
to follow the sound...
of what must be the music
of magical sprites,
singing and strumming
and dancing all night?

You wind through a forest of branches and brambles.

The woods are awake, making way for your rambles.

you search and you search
till you just can't see straight,
only turning back home
when the hour grows late.

"Are they out there?" you wonder, curled up in your bed.

The fairies' reply
is right on your head.